THE USBORNE BOOK pop-ups

Richard Dungworth and Ray Gibson

Designed by Rachel Wells

Edited by Cheryl Lanyon
Illustrated by Teri Gower
Photographs by Howard Allman
Managing designer: Mary Cartwright

Contents

Getting started

Most of the pop-ups in this book are fairly quick and easy to make. As the book goes on, the projects get slightly more difficult, so it's a good idea to try some of the early ones first. When a project involves marking out special pieces, you'll find outlines, called templates, that you can trace from the book. These pages give you some handy tips before you start.

Use different kinds of paper to make your pop-ups look good.

What will I need?

You'll find a list at the beginning of each project telling you what you need. Read it carefully to find out the correct equipment and sizes of paper or cardboard.

How to trace a template

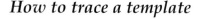

Don't forget to trace all the details.

1. Lay a piece of tracing paper over the template. Hold it in place with paper clips. Trace over the outline with a pencil.

2. Unclip the tracing paper and turn it over. Scribble thickly over the back of the outline with a soft-leaded pencil.

Press hard to transfer the outline.

3. Turn the tracing over again. Clip it over the paper you want to trace onto. Go over the outline with a ballpoint pen.

Half templates

Red edge

When you're tracing a half template onto a folded piece of paper, make sure you line up the red edge with the fold.

Folding tips

Whenever you make a fold, follow these tips to keep it neat and accurate:

1. Work on a firm, flat surface.

2. Fold the paper away from you if possible.

3. Make sure any edges or corners that should meet do so before you crease the fold.

4. To crease the fold, smooth along it from the middle to the ends.

Gluing on glitter or sequins will add sparkle to your backing cards.

You'll need paper clips to hold tracings in position.

Scoring cardboard

Where the book says to use thick paper, you can use very thin cardboard instead, but you'll need to score any lines before you fold them so that you get a neat fold. Score lines with an old ballpoint pen that has run out of ink.

Use a ruler to score straight lines.

Adding a backing card

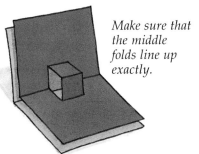

Make sure that the middle folds line up exactly.

For some of the projects you will need to glue your pop-up inside a backing card. Be careful not to get glue behind any of the pop-up parts.

Making a pop-up book

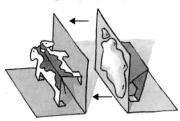

You can turn your cards into pages of a pop-up book. Make several cards of the same size and glue them back-to-back.

Finishing touches

Try to make the outside of your pop-up cards look as good as possible too. Draw or glue on decorations, and add a message.

This book is made from the pop-up farm animal cards on page 14.

3

Easy pop-ups

Stand-up cutout

You will need: a picture cut from a magazine; a piece of thick, bright paper, slightly larger than your picture; a pencil; a ruler; scissors; glue.

This type of card works best if you use a picture with a tall part that sticks up above the rest.

If you like, you can draw a picture at step 2, rather than gluing one on.

Use a craft knife to begin the cut, or carefully push a scissor point through.

1. Make a mark halfway along each of the paper's long edges. Rule a pencil line to join the two marks.

2. Glue your picture onto the paper, so that the part that you want to pop up is above the pencil line.

3. Cut around the part of the picture above the line. The red line on the picture above shows where to cut.

4. Fold back the top part of the paper around the picture. Crease it along the line that you drew in step 1.

4

Hippo ballerina

This hippopotamus ballet dancer has a pop-up ballet skirt.
You will need: a piece of pink paper 20 x 10cm (8 x 4in); a piece of thick, white paper 19 x 19cm (7$\frac{1}{2}$ x 7$\frac{1}{2}$in); a pencil; felt-tip pens; glue.

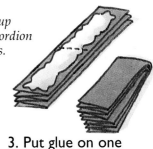

You'll end up with an accordion fold like this.

1. Lay the pink paper with its long edges at the sides. Fold down a 2cm (³/₄in) strip at the top edge.

2. Turn the paper over and fold down another 2cm (³/₄in). Repeat this step until you run out of paper.

3. Put glue on one side of the strip. Fold it in half so that its ends meet. Press while the glue dries.

4. Fold the piece of white paper in half to make a card. Draw a hippo ballerina across the inside of the fold.

5. Glue the accordion strip onto your ballerina, so that its folded end is against the middle crease.

If it is easier, you can copy or trace this hippo at step 4.

6. Put some glue on top of the strip and carefully close the card. Press down while the glue dries.

7. When you open the card, the pink accordion-folded strip will fan out like a ballet skirt.

You could draw a different kind of animal, or a human character.

5

Things on springs

These pop-ups are based on an easy-to-make paper spring. **You will need:** two strips of thick paper, one yellow and one red, both 3 x 50cm (1¼ x 20in); white cardboard 3.5 x 3.5cm (1½ x 1½in); glue; scissors; felt-tip pens; a small gift box, about 4 x 4 x 4cm (1½ x 1½ x 1½in). If you don't have a suitable gift box, you can find out how to make your own on page 32.

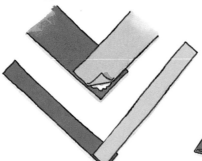

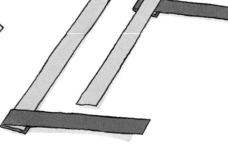

1. Glue the end of the yellow strip over the end of the red one, so that they make a right angle. Lay the strips so that they are in a V-shape.

2. Fold the red strip across the edge of the yellow strip and crease. Then fold the yellow strip down across the red strip in the same way.

Carefully push your spring inside its box and close the lid. It will pop up when the box is opened.

Trim off
the extra
paper here.

Tab

3. Continue folding the red and yellow strips across one another so that they build up into a spring. Keep going until you run out of paper.

4. Glue down the last whole yellow flap and trim it to size. Fold over the extra paper on the red strip to make a tab, as shown in the picture.

5. Draw a picture on the white cardboard and cut it out. Glue it to the tab. Glue the other end of the spring to the bottom of the gift box.

Make longer springs by using longer strips, or by gluing several springs end to end.

Try out different pop-up pictures, like this custard pie, or jumping flea.

Draw presents or balloons on the backing card of a birthday cake chain.

Pop-up chains

These pop-up cards are made from simple paper chains. The snowman chain makes an ideal Christmas card.

For the snowman card, you will need: a piece of white paper 20 x 10cm (8 x 4in); a piece of thick blue paper 20 x 13cm (8 x 5in); a strip of white paper 20 x 4cm (8 x 1½in); a pencil; scissors; felt-tip pens; glue.

1. Fold the white paper in half so that its short edges meet. Fold back each of these edges in turn to meet the first fold. This makes a zigzag fold.

2. Keeping the paper folded, draw an outline of a snowman on it in pencil. Make sure that his arms and his toes touch the sides of the paper.

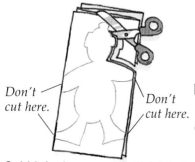

Don't cut here.   *Don't cut here.*

3. With the paper still folded, cut around your snowman. Don't cut around the ends of his arms and toes, as these will be the links in the chain.

4. Unfold the paper carefully. Lay it flat, with any pencil markings on the back. Use felt-tip pens to draw faces, hats and scarves on the snowmen.

5. To make a backing card, fold the blue paper so that its short edges meet. Unfold and lay it flat. Put glue on the back of the first and last snowmen.

8

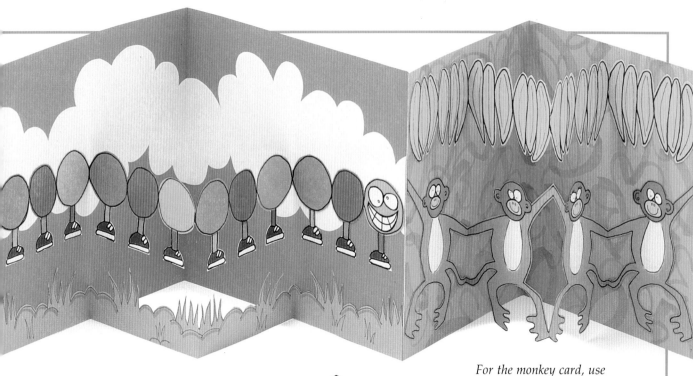

For the monkey card, use yellow paper to make the chain of bananas.

6. Lay the chain across the backing card, making sure that the middle folds line up. Press the end snowmen down until the glue is dry.

Different chains

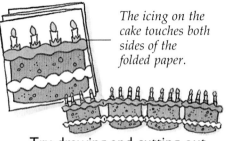

The icing on the cake touches both sides of the folded paper.

Try drawing and cutting out different outlines at steps 2 and 3. Whatever you draw, it must touch both sides so that it will make a chain.

7. Carefully close the card, pulling the middle fold of the snowman chain toward you. When you open it, the middle two snowmen will stand out.

8. For snowy grass, fold the thin strip of paper into a zigzag fold. Draw and cut a grassy outline along the top. Glue it inside the card as before.

You can copy or trace these outlines at step 2 to make the monkey or snowman cards.

Boxfold cards

One of the easiest ways to make something pop up from a flat card is to use a special fold called a boxfold. This floating spaceman is just one of the many things you could glue to the front of a boxfold. **You will need:** two pieces of thick dark blue paper 22 x 11cm (8½ x 4¼in); thick white paper 6 x 6cm (2½ x 2½in); felt-tip pens; scissors; glue; a silver pen.

You could add a rocket on a tiny paper spring. Make the spring as on page 6, but use thinner, shorter strips.

  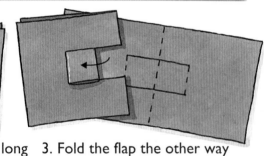

1. Fold one of the pieces of blue paper in half so that its short edges meet. Make a pencil mark 4cm (1½in) from each end of the folded edge.

2. Rule a line 4cm (1½in) long from each mark, at right angles to the folded edge. Cut along both lines. Fold over the flap between the cuts.

3. Fold the flap the other way to crease it in the opposite direction. Unfold the flap and open the card. Lay it flat, with any pencil marks facing down.

You can copy or trace this spaceman at step 7, if you like.

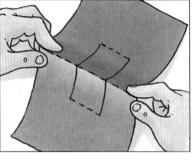

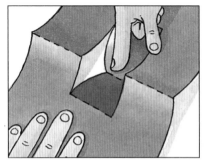

4. Pinch along the middle fold on either side of the flap to crease it the other way. Only do this at the ends of the fold, not on the flap part.

5. Push the flap down with your finger, as shown. Close the card carefully and smooth it flat. When you open it, the flap will pop up to make a box shape.

Make sure the middle folds line up.

Don't get glue behind the boxfold.

Draw or glue on stars

6. Fold the other piece of blue paper to make a backing card. Put glue on the back of the first piece of paper and press it inside the backing card.

7. Draw a spaceman on the piece of white cardboard. Use felt-tip pens to fill in his spacesuit and face. Carefully cut around him.

8. Glue your spaceman onto the front of the pop-up box so that he looks as if he's floating in space. Decorate the inside of the card with silver stars.

3-D boxfold scenes

Make the middle box the biggest.

By changing the length of the cuts at step 2, you can make different-sized boxfolds. For a 3-D scene, make three sizes of box and glue a picture to each.

For a Christmas scene, glue a cut-out fir tree to the middle box. Decorate the smaller boxes like presents. Add stars in the background.

To make an underwater scene, glue seaweed shapes to the side boxes and a submarine to the middle one. Add a sea-horse on a tiny paper spring.

Cancan legs

These animal cancan dancers have high-kicking pop-up legs, and are good for a celebration. Their legs work in a similar way to the boxfold for the spaceman card on page 10.

To make the bears, you will need: two pieces of thick yellow paper 15 x 15cm (6 x 6in); a ruler; a pencil; scissors; felt-tip pens; glue; a paper doily; glitter.

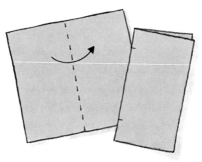

1. Fold one of the pieces of yellow paper in half. Make a pencil mark on the folded edge, 3cm (1¼in) from each end of the fold.

2. Rule a line 2.5cm (1in) long from each mark, at right angles to the folded edge. Cut along both lines. Fold over the flap between the cuts.

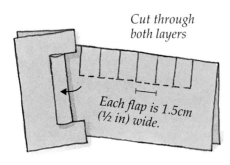

Cut through both layers

Each flap is 1.5cm (½ in) wide.

3. Fold and crease the flap in the other direction, then lay it flat. Rule five more lines to divide the flap into six equal strips. Cut along each line.

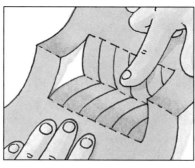

4. Open the card and lay it flat, with any pencil marks facing down. Lift it into a tent shape, pushing down the six flaps. Each flap makes a leg.

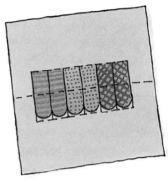

5. Lay the card flat again, this time with any marks facing up. Draw a curve for a paw at the end of each leg. Fill in the legs with three pairs of fancy tights.

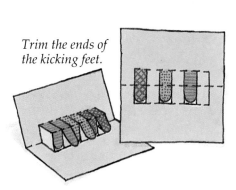

Trim the ends of the kicking feet.

6. Snip across the base of every other leg so that they can lift up. Turn the card over and draw tights on the back of each kicking leg.

For extra razzmatazz, add stars, glitter, and silver foil headdresses.

Decorate the doily petticoats with felt-tip pens and glitter.

Don't get glue behind the legs.

7. Fold the second piece of paper to make a backing card. Glue your pop-up inside the backing card, making sure that you line up the folds.

8. Draw a bear's head about 2cm (¾in) above each pair of legs. Add a face and ears. Give each bear two arms, sticking up in the air.

9. For petticoats, cut pieces from the paper doily. Cut curved sections with a straight snip across the bottom. Glue them above each pair of legs.

Cancan cat chorus

For this card, use a piece of thick paper 16 x 50cm (6¼ x 20in). Fold the long edges together. Follow steps 1 and 2 to measure and mark out the card. At step 3, cut 24 legs, each 1.5cm (½in) wide. At steps 5 and 8 draw cats' paws, faces and arms.

13

Pop-up farm

This 3-D cow folds flat inside a card. You can make other farm animals in the same way. **For the cow, you will need**: thick green paper 18 x 12cm (7 x 4³/₄in); thick white paper 15 x 9cm (6 x 3¹/₂in); pink paper 6.5 x 2cm (2¹/₂ x ³/₄in); a black felt-tip pen; black yarn; a pencil; a ruler; scissors; glue.

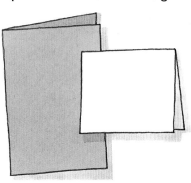

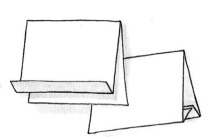

1. Fold the pieces of green and white paper in half so that their short edges meet. Lay the white paper so that the fold runs along the top.

2. Using a ruler, draw a line 1cm (¹/₂in) from the bottom of the white paper. Fold along the line both ways to crease it. Do the same on the other side.

3. Draw an outline of a cow on the folded paper. Make sure that its back runs along the fold and that both its feet touch the crease, as shown.

Tabs

4. Mark a tab at the end of both legs, as shown. With the paper still folded, cut out the cow, leaving the tabs. Add cow markings to both sides.

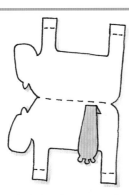

5. Cut an udder shape, like the one shown here, at one end of the pink paper. Fold over a 1cm (1/2in) tab at the other end and put glue on it.

6. Unfold the cow. Lay it flat, decorated side down. Press on the udder tab, so that its fold runs along the inside of the middle fold.

For a hen, make the tail feathers and comb touch the fold at step 3.

Tape the tail behind the udders.

7. For a tail, cut a 5cm (2in) strand of yarn and tape one end inside the crease. Fold the cow. Put glue on both tabs on the side facing up.

8. Turn the cow over and press the glued tabs along the crease on the green backing card as shown. Put glue on the cow's other two tabs.

9. Carefully close the card and press down while the glue dries. When you open the card, the cow will stand up and its udders will dangle.

Make other animals by drawing a different outline at step 3.

For a farmyard scene, make lots of animal cards. Cut grass shapes from green paper and glue them on.

Butterflies and bats

These butterflies and bats spread their wings as you open them. If you have a party, you can use them as place cards.

For a butterfly, you will need: a piece of thick pale paper 8 x 6cm (3¼ x 2½in); a pencil; scissors; paints. **For a bat, you will need:** a piece of thick black paper 8 x 6cm (3¼ x 2½in); a pencil; scissors.

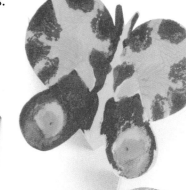

Butterfly template

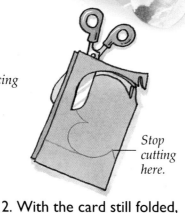

Making a butterfly

Position your tracing like this.

Stop cutting here.

1. Fold the pale paper in half so that its short edges meet. Trace the butterfly template onto it. Make sure you line up the red edge with the fold.

2. With the card still folded, cut along the curved outline of the wings, starting at the antennae. Don't cut along the diagonal fold line.

3. Make a straight cut from the side of the card to the lower edge of the wing. This will cut away the top part of the card around the butterfly.

Bat template

On a bat card, write the name in silver or gold pen.

4. Fold over the butterfly along the diagonal line, first in one direction and then the other, so that the fold is well creased. Open up the card.

5. Hold the card so that the pencil-marked side is facing you. Close it carefully, pushing the cutout part down inside the card, as shown.

Making a bat

Write your guest's name along the base.

This makes the same pattern on both wings.

6. Close the card completely and smooth it flat to crease all the folds. Add a name. When you open the card, the butterfly will spread its wings.

7. Dab small blobs of bright paint on the top of one wing. Close the card and press the wings together. Open the card again and leave it to dry.

You can make a bat in the same way. Fold the black paper in half and trace the bat template onto it. Then follow steps 2-6 for the butterfly.

17

Animal mouths

You can use the technique on these pages to make pop-up mouths for all kinds of animals, from wide-mouthed frogs to sharp-toothed dogs. **For the frog, you will need:** a piece of pale green paper 16 x 14cm (6¼ x 5½in); same size piece of thick, red paper; white paper; a pencil; a ruler; glue; felt-tip pens.

1. Fold the green paper in half so that its short edges meet. Draw a pencil line 4cm (1½in) long, halfway up the folded edge. Cut along the line.

2. Make pencil marks on the folded edge 2.5cm (1in) above and below the cut. Draw a diagonal line from the end of the cut to each mark.

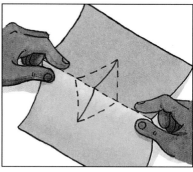

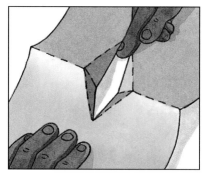

3. Fold along both lines to make two triangular flaps. Unfold the flaps, turn the paper over and fold them in the other direction. Unfold.

4. Open out the paper and lay it flat with any pencil marks face down. Pinch the ends of the middle fold to crease them the other way.

5. Use one of your fingers to push down both triangular flaps. This will make a diamond-shaped hole, as shown in the picture.

For a beak, cut a shorter, slightly curved line at step 1.

Try making a puffin, peacock, or hatching chick.

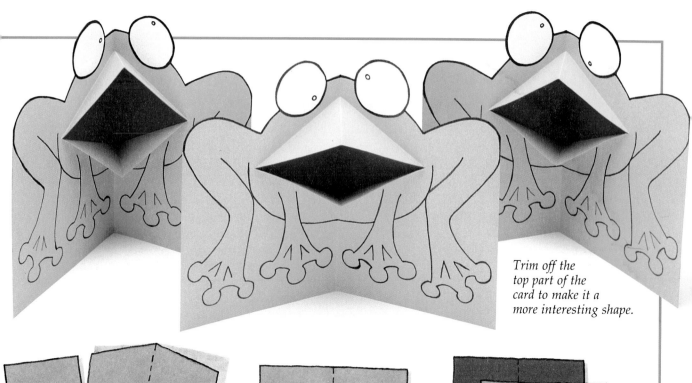

Trim off the top part of the card to make it a more interesting shape.

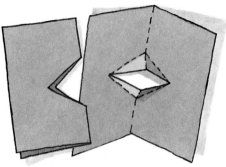

6. Carefully close the card and smooth over it to flatten the triangular flaps inside. When you open it up, the flaps will close together like a mouth.

7. Draw a frog around the mouth. Draw a fat body, long legs and webbed feet. Cut out and glue on two circles of white paper for bulging eyes.

8. Fold the red cardboard and glue it on as a backing card. Make sure that the folds line up, and that you don't get glue behind the frog's mouth.

For sharp-toothed jaws like these, cut a zig-zag line at step 1.

Spaceship lift-off

As you open this card, the spaceship inside swings up as though it is taking off. The backing card is covered with 3-D craters. You'll find templates for the spaceship and its smoke cloud on page 30.

You will need: a piece of thick yellow paper 20 x 18cm (8 x 7in); two pieces of thick white paper 15 x 8cm (6 x 3in) and 19 x 5cm (7½ x 2in); a pencil; a ruler; scissors; glue; felt-tip pens; coins.

1. Fold the yellow paper so its short edges meet. Unfold. Mark 5cm (2in) and 7.5cm (3in) down the crease.

2. Using a ruler, draw pencil lines from each mark to both top corners of the paper, to make two V-shapes.

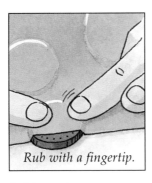

Rub with a fingertip.

3. To make craters, turn the paper over and slip a coin under it. Rub over the coin to make each crater.

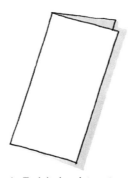

4. Fold the big piece of white paper in half, so that its long edges meet. Lay it with the fold on the left.

5. Trace the spaceship template onto the paper, making sure that you line up the red edge with the fold.

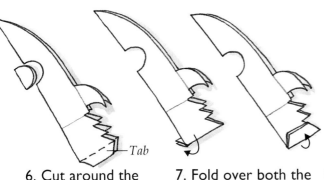

—Tab

6. Cut around the spaceship, flames and tab. For a porthole, cut a small semi-circle from the fold.

7. Fold over both the tabs along the dotted line. Fold them both ways so that they are well creased.

8. Unfold the spaceship and decorate both sides. Add a border around the porthole and bright flames.

Put the glue here.

9. Partly close the spaceship and fold over both tabs as shown. Put some glue on the underside of each tab.

10. Press the spaceship onto the backing card, so that the tabs fit along the inside of the top pencil V-shape.

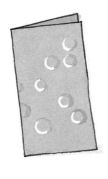

11. Close the card carefully and press while the glue dries. When you open it, the spaceship will rise up.

Crease the tabs along the dotted line.

12. For the smoke, fold the white paper in half. Trace the smoke cloud template onto it and cut it out.

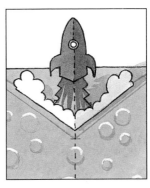

13. Glue the smoke cloud inside the card in the same way as the spaceship, but along the bottom V-shape.

Crazy crocodiles

Make these pop-up jaws and draw a crazy crocodile around them. You can copy one of the ones on the opposite page, or make up your own. **You will need:** a piece of thick pale paper 24 x 20cm (9½ x 8in); two pieces of green paper, each 11 x 8cm (4¼ x 3in); a pencil; a ruler; scissors; glue; felt-tip pens.

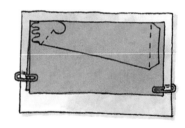

Only cut to here.

1. Fold one of the pieces of green paper in half, so that its long edges meet. Trace the top jaw template against the fold and cut out the jaw.

2. For the crocodile's nose, cut along the curved line. Fold the ends of the jaw along the dotted lines. Fold them both ways so they are well creased.

The nose will stick up.

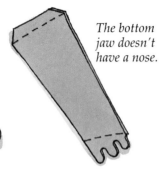

The bottom jaw doesn't have a nose.

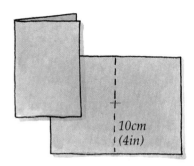

10cm (4in)

3. Unfold the jaw. Lay it with any pencil marks facing down. Lift it into a tent shape, pushing in the flap at the nose end. Carefully close and flatten it.

4. Make the crocodile's bottom jaw in the same way as the top jaw, using the other piece of green paper and the top jaw template.

5. Fold the piece of pale paper in half so that its short edges meet. Open it out. Make a pencil mark on the crease 10cm (4in) from the bottom.

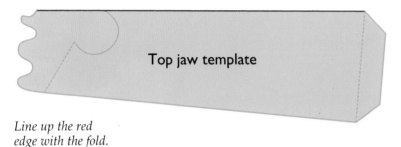

Top jaw template

Line up the red edge with the fold.

Bottom jaw template

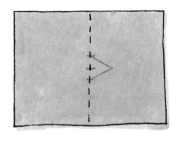

6. Make marks on the crease 2cm (³/₄in) above and below the first mark. Make a fourth mark 2.5cm (1in) to the right of the first. Join them up as shown.

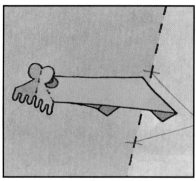

7. Glue the right-hand tab of the top jaw along the top edge of the triangle on the backing card. The top edge of the jaw must touch the crease.

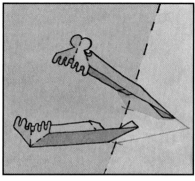

8. Glue the bottom jaw, the other way up, to the right-hand side of the card in the same way. Line it up with the bottom edge of the triangle.

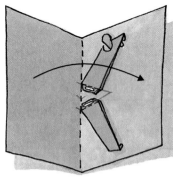

9. Lay the jaws, folded flat, across the right-hand side of the backing card. Put glue on the tabs on both jaws. Close the card carefully and press.

Paint the teeth white.

Aztec temple

You can make a simple pop-up more impressive by adding extra pop-up parts inside some of its folds. The Aztec temple and wedding cake cards on this page are made from boxfolds within boxfolds.

For the temple you will need: two pieces of yellow paper, both 17 x 10cm (6¾ x 4in); a ruler; a pencil; scissors; glue; felt-tip pens.

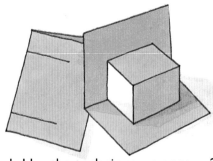

1. Use the technique on page 10 to make a pop-up boxfold. To get the size of box you need, make 4cm (1½in) cuts, 2cm (¾in) from either end.

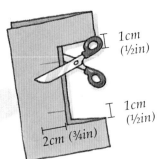

2. Close the card, with the box folded flat inside. Mark out and cut a second boxfold, along the fold of the first, as shown in the picture.

Pinch the boxfolds to crease them.

3. Crease the new flaps in both directions. Unfold them and open the card. Carefully push the flaps through to make two more pop-up boxes.

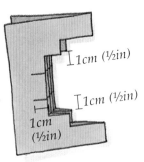

4. Close the card again and smooth it flat. Mark out a third boxfold, as shown in the picture. Cut through all the layers to make four new flaps.

Decorate the temple.

5. Fold and unfold the flaps so they are well creased. Open the card and carefully push through the small boxes. Fold and glue on a backing card.

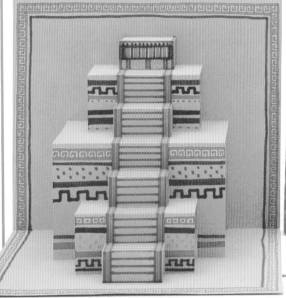

For a wedding cake card, use white paper.

Glue extra pieces to the boxfolds to make the bottom tier and third tier of the cake.

Decorate the lower boxfolds like presents.

Surprise!

As you open this card, the pop-up hands give you a present. Follow the steps to make the hands, then draw a background around them. You'll find the templates on page 30.
You will need: a piece of pink paper 10 x 10cm (4 x 4in); a piece of yellow paper 9 x 9cm (3½ x 3½in); a piece of white paper 18 x 18cm (7 x 7in); glue; a pencil; a ruler; scissors; pens.

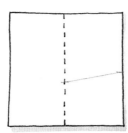

1. Fold all the pieces of paper in half. Trace the present template onto the yellow piece and the hand template onto the pink piece. Cut them out.

2. Unfold the white paper. Make marks 8.5cm (3¼in) up the right-hand side, and 7cm (2¾in) up the crease. Draw a pencil line to join the marks.

3. Unfold the present and decorate both sides. Fold the present again and fold up both its tabs. Put some glue on each tab as shown.

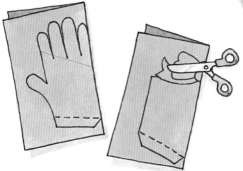

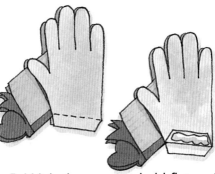

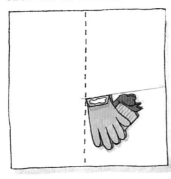

4. Glue the present onto the left hand (the one with the diagonal line on) as shown, so that its runs along the line and meets the crease in the hands.

5. With the present held flat, carefully fold over the other hand and press it down. Fold up the tabs on both hands and put some glue on them.

6. Glue the left hand onto the backing card, so that its tab runs along the pencil line and meets the middle fold. Close the card carefully and press.

Moving robot

Pop-up books often have tabs to pull, flaps to lift, and parts to slide. This robot model lets you try making some of these tabs, flaps and sliders.

The control button on your robot's side slides up and down.

You will need:
thick paper 40 x 25cm (16 x 10in); thin white cardboard 25 x 10cm (10 x 4in); a pencil; a ruler; glue; scissors; a craft knife; felt-tip pens; two paper fasteners. You'll find all the templates for the robot on pages 30 and 31.

Using a craft knife

You'll need to use a craft knife to cut the holes and slots in the robot's body and slider pieces. Work on top of an old magazine or some thick cardboard. Keep your fingers clear of the blade.

By pushing and pulling your robot's legs, you can make his arms wave and his eyes and mouth open and shut. The display on his tummy will move as well.

When you lift the flap on your robot's chest a coil of cable pops up.

Robot instructions

Holes

Slots

1. Trace the templates for the robot's body, front, legs, arm and back of head onto the paper. Trace the arm twice. Cut out all the pieces.

2. On the body piece, cut out the holes for the mouth and eyes, and the two thin slots. Use a sharp pencil to make two small holes as marked.

3. Trace the slider template onto cardboard and cut it out. Cut out the rectangular holes and the two small slots marked on the slider piece.

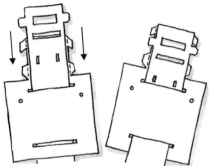

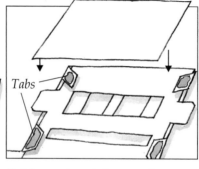

Tabs

Decorate the rest of the face.

4. Slip the end of the slider without the holes through the top slot in the body, and back up through the lower slot, as shown in the picture.

5. Move the slider so the top hole lines up with the eyes. Fold over the tabs above and below the ears. Glue the back of the head onto the tabs.

6. Turn the robot over. Make sure the slider is pushed up, so that the eyelids are open. Draw an eye in each eye hole, and teeth inside the mouth.

Fill in the robot's legs and big metal boots.

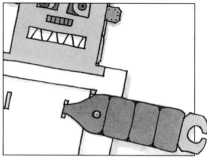

7. Decorate the legs. Put glue on the slider where it sticks out below the body. Press on the leg piece in the position shown by the dotted line.

8. Decorate both of the arm pieces. Use the point of a sharp pencil to make a small hole in each arm, as marked on the template.

9. Slip the thin end of one arm into the right-hand slot on the slider, as shown here. Line up the hole in the arm with the hole in the body.

28

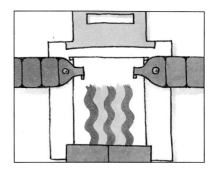

10. Push a paper fastener through the holes in the arm and body. Turn the robot over and open the fastener behind the robot's back.

11. Slip the robot's other arm into the left-hand slot in the slider. Fix it in position with a paper fastener in the same way as before.

12. Use felt-tip pens to draw a bright zigzag pattern running down the slider, from below the arm slots to the top edge of the leg piece.

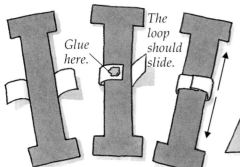

Glue here.

The loop should slide.

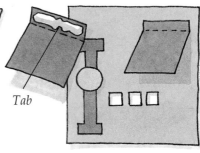

Tab

13. Trace the I-bar template onto thick paper and cut it out. Cut a strip of paper 3 x 1cm (1¼ x ½in) and use it to make a loop around the bar.

14. Put glue under both ends of the I-bar and glue it to the front piece. Cut a small circle of cardboard and glue it onto the sliding loop for a button.

15. Cut a piece of thick paper 5 x 4cm (2 x 1½in). Fold one short end to make a 1cm (½in) tab. Unfold the tab and glue it to the front piece as shown.

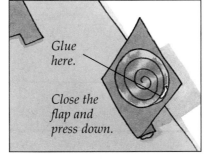

Glue here.

Close the flap and press down.

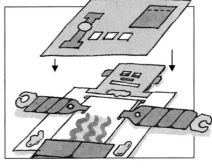

16. Draw a spiral on a 4 x 4cm (1½ x 1½in) square of paper. Trim around it, then carefully cut along the spiral line to make a snake-like coil.

17. Glue the middle of the coil to the underside of the flap on the front piece. Put some glue on the outer end of the coil and close the flap.

18. Cut out the square holes on the front piece. Put glue at the bottom corners of the body and under the chin. Press on the front to finish the robot.

Templates

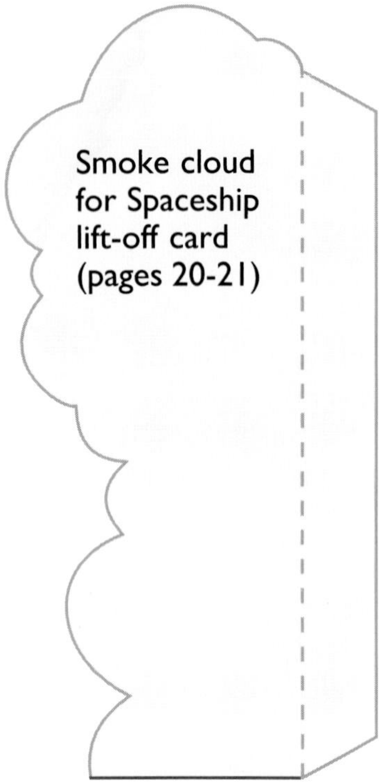

Smoke cloud
for Spaceship
lift-off card
(pages 20-21)

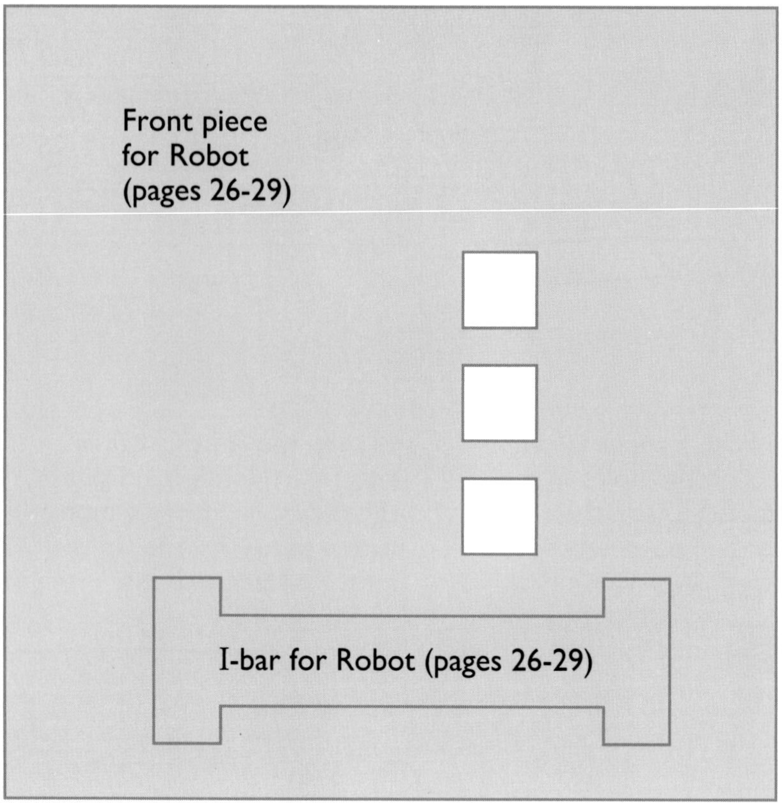

Front piece
for Robot
(pages 26-29)

I-bar for Robot (pages 26-29)

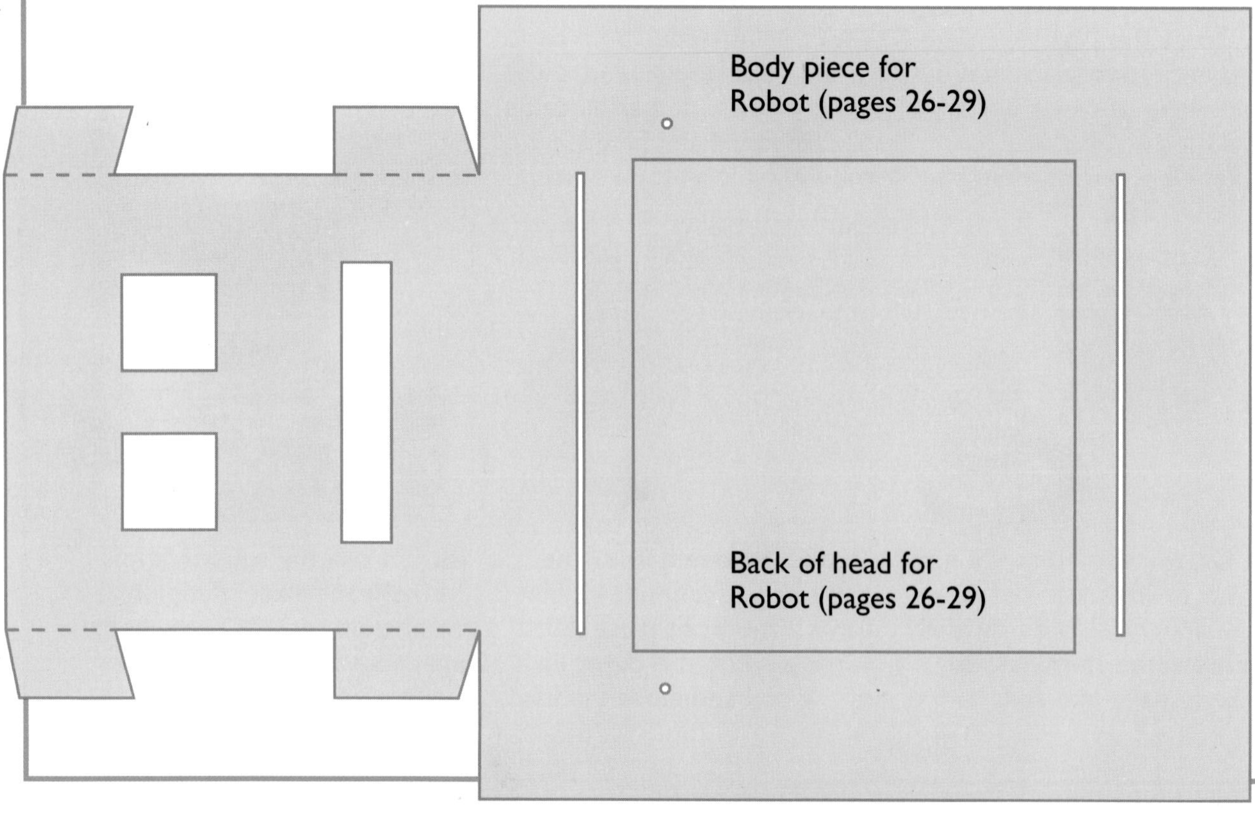

Body piece for
Robot (pages 26-29)

Back of head for
Robot (pages 26-29)

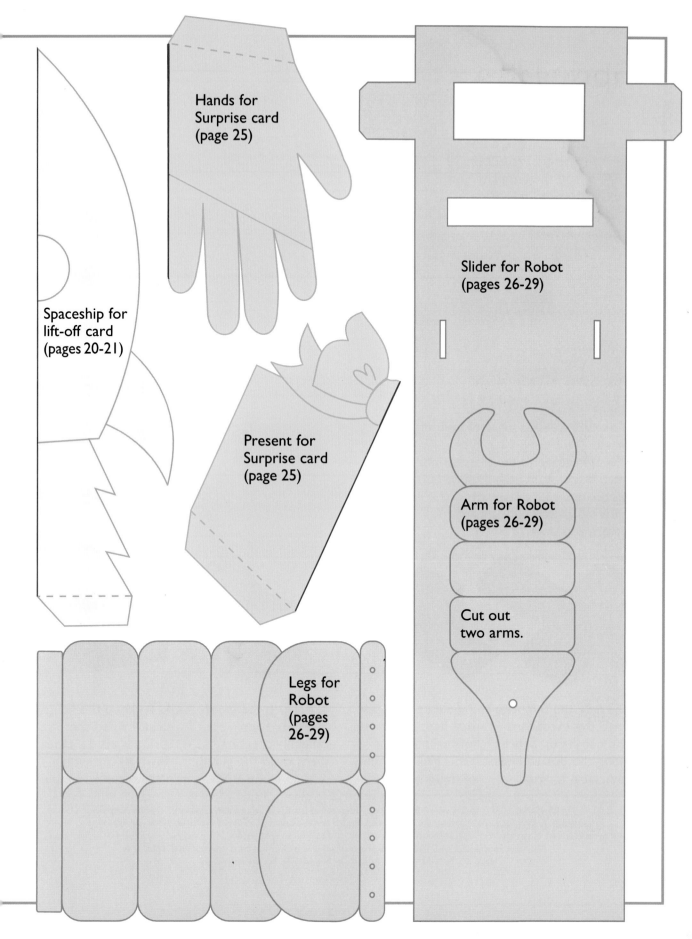

Hands for
Surprise card
(page 25)

Spaceship for
lift-off card
(pages 20-21)

Present for
Surprise card
(page 25)

Slider for Robot
(pages 26-29)

Arm for Robot
(pages 26-29)

Cut out
two arms.

Legs for
Robot
(pages
26-29)

Spring box

If you need to make a box for the pop-up project on page 4, use the template and instructions on this page.

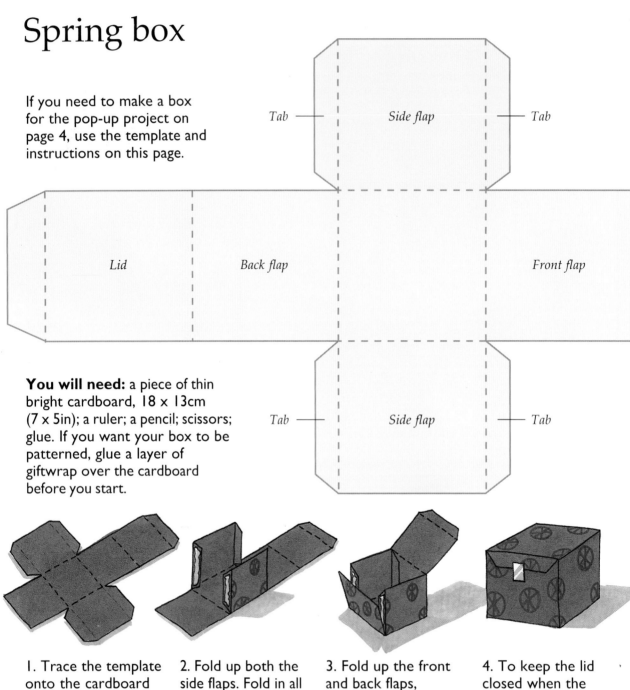

Tab — *Side flap* — *Tab*

Lid | *Back flap* | *Front flap*

Tab — *Side flap* — *Tab*

You will need: a piece of thin bright cardboard, 18 x 13cm (7 x 5in); a ruler; a pencil; scissors; glue. If you want your box to be patterned, glue a layer of giftwrap over the cardboard before you start.

1. Trace the template onto the cardboard and cut it out. Score along the dotted lines, then turn it over.

2. Fold up both the side flaps. Fold in all four tabs and put some glue on each of them as shown.

3. Fold up the front and back flaps, carefully pressing them onto the glued tabs to make a box.

4. To keep the lid closed when the spring is inside, tape down its tab with a piece of masking tape.

First published in 1997 by Usborne Publishing Ltd., Usborne House, 83-85 Saffron Hill, London EC1N 8RT, England.
Copyright © 1997 Usborne Publishing Ltd. The name Usborne and the device🎈 are Trade marks of Usborne Publishing Ltd.
UE. First published in America in August1997. Printed in Portugal.